Steve Parish

Millicent's MUDDLE

Written by
Rebecca Johnson

Images by
Steve Parish

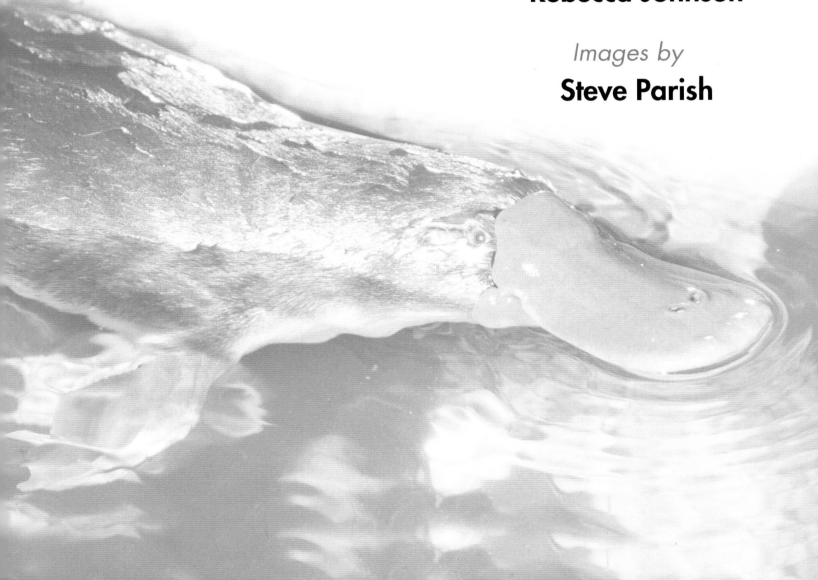

Millicent was a platypus. She lived in a waterhole all by herself. Her burrow was a long, dark tunnel that opened out to the edge of the clear water. She had lived in the same burrow for her entire life, and she loved it.

Hardly any of the animals that visited the waterhole to drink even knew she existed. As soon as she heard a twig crack or leaves rustle, she would slip silently into the cool, clear depths of the water and hide until they had left.

Millicent was too afraid to meet any of the animals that shared her waterhole. She had seen her reflection in the water's surface and knew that she was completely different from all of them. She was afraid they might laugh at her if she tried to talk to them.

As she lay in her burrow, she would hear them chatting and laughing amongst themselves as they drank and splashed at the edge of the water, and she felt terribly lonely. But, she never let them know that she was there.

 There was one kingfisher, though, who visited the waterhole every afternoon. Some days he'd swoop down so suddenly that Millicent would be caught completely off guard and, seeing her, he would try to start up a conversation.

"Nice day, isn't it?" he might ask, but Millicent was very nervous and would quickly turn her back on him and scurry into her burrow, not answering at all.

Sometimes, once safe inside her home, she would feel awful for being so rude to the kingfisher. But it had been so long since she had talked to anyone, she was afraid she might say something really silly, so it was better to say nothing at all.

Things continued as they were for a very long time. Millicent kept completely to herself, and the kingfisher gave up trying to talk to her.

Then, one day, something dreadful happened.

Millicent had been swimming along the muddy bottom of the waterhole for quite some time hunting for worms. She caught a particularly large one and stashed it neatly in her cheek pouch. As she rose to the surface to eat it, a loud splashing noise caught her attention.

Millicent could not believe her eyes. There was a large platypus making a great show of cleaning himself right in front of her burrow. There was much scratching and preening and rolling over in the water going on.

Silently, Millicent hid herself in amongst the leaves of a tree whose branches overhung the waterhole and watched in amazement.

Without so much as a backward glance, the intruder, once finally satisfied with his appearance, marched straight into Millicent's lovely burrow.

"Oh no!" thought Millicent. "What is happening here? Someone has moved into my home without asking. Oh dear, what am I going to do?"

She lay quietly in the water for a very long time, watching and waiting, all the time feeling more and more anxious.

She felt like paddling over and demanding that he leave. She felt like storming into her burrow and frightening the living daylights out of him. But she did nothing.

How could she? She couldn't even talk to a friendly kingfisher. How could she be brave enough to scare away a stranger?

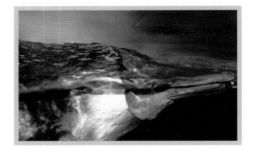

So Millicent said nothing and did nothing, but became sadder and sadder . . . and colder and colder.

By nightfall, the rude platypus was curled up snugly in her burrow. Millicent felt very sorry for herself as she snuffled amongst the rocks, looking for somewhere to sleep. She had never slept out of her burrow before, and sleep she did not. All night the noises around her kept her awake and she feared that a dingo or goanna might sneak up on her.

By the next morning, Millicent was very upset. But she remained hidden and did not voice her feelings.

The day passed slowly and the situation did not improve.

Late in the afternoon, the kingfisher landed on a branch just above her head.

Millicent froze, feeling even more unsure of herself.

The kingfisher sat completely still and watched the small fish swimming among the reeds along the bank. Then, in the shadows, he saw Millicent. Their eyes locked for a moment and she cringed as she slowly backed a little further away, turning her gaze from him.

The kingfisher looked from Millicent to her burrow.

"It looks like you have a visitor," he said.

"Visitors don't just come and take over your home," Millicent whispered, trying very hard not to cry. "Visitors wait until they are invited."

"Have you told him how you feel?" asked the kingfisher, as Millicent slipped into the water.

Millicent looked up angrily, for she was sure he was making fun of her, but she saw concern in the bird's eyes.

"I couldn't possibly do that," replied Millicent, shaking her head slowly.

"Why not?" The kingfisher was puzzled.

"I'm not very good at telling others how I feel," she said, her voice quivering. "I'm sure they would make fun of me."

"But you're talking to me, when before you were afraid to. I think you will find most animals are quite friendly, if you take the chance to get to know them."

To this Millicent simply shrugged her shoulders. The two sat in silence for some time, watching the other platypus.

"You are so brave," she said hopefully. "Maybe you could go over and tell him the burrow is mine, and chase him away?"

The kingfisher sat and thought for a moment. Eventually, he spoke. "I could go over there and chase that fellow away," he said, "but I can't stay here all day and keep him away. Why don't you go over and talk to him yourself?"

"But it's not fair," cried the little platypus. "I have lived in that burrow all my life and this is my waterhole. He can't ...."

"Go and talk to him," the kingfisher butted in calmly. "Are you more worried about being embarrassed or about losing your home? Sometimes you have to take a risk to defend something you really care about."

"I knew you wouldn't help me," she wept, and, turning her back on him, she slipped silently away.

So Millicent spent another cold night on the bank, gazing at her lovely home with great sadness.

The next day she awoke to the sound of earth works at the entrance to her burrow. Every few minutes the intruder would emerge, sending great clods of dirt into the water with his leathery bill.

"My burrow," she squealed, and, without a second thought, she shot through the water and came to the surface just inches from the startled platypus's bill.

She opened her mouth to yell at him but the only sound which emerged was a high pitched little whimper.

"My goodness!" gasped the male platypus, filled with concern. "Are you all right?" He pushed little Millicent protectively behind him and scanned the water for danger.

"What is it? What's the matter?" he worried, taking her hand into his own.

Millicent trembled all over and started to cry. "This is my burrow. . . my mother built this. I have lived here all my life. You can't come in here uninvited and start moving things around! You can't ..."

"Oh, dear me," stammered the big platypus, "I am *so* sorry! I had no idea this was your burrow. I asked all the other animals and they said they had never seen anyone here, so I assumed it was empty. I cannot tell you how embarrassed I am. I will do everything I can to put it back the way it was."

He started frantically replacing the rocks and soil at the entrance, at the same time explaining that the water in his waterhole upstream had dried up because of the drought. He had been heading downstream when he found this splendid burrow and, for all he could see, it was completely empty.

"Oh, if only you had come and talked to me," he cried, "I would never have been so rude as to take someone else's home deliberately."

With that the poor fellow left the waterhole, apologising frantically whilst scampering clumsily across the rocks.

Millicent's bill was still open, as he had taken her completely by surprise. She looked up to see the kingfisher watching from a nearby tree, and she realised how unreasonable she had been.

"I'm sorry," she called after the other platypus. "Truly, I am. Please forgive me for being so rude. I should have told you how I was feeling straight away.

"How could you have known? I am sure there is room in this waterhole for both of us – if you felt that you could share with me, that is?"

The male platypus turned and smiled. "That's really nice of you," he said, slipping into the cool water. "Thank you."

Then, pausing, he added shyly, "Perhaps you might even let me bring you some lunch one day?"